This book belongs to

....

....

A catalogue record for this book is available from the British Library
Published by Ladybird Books Ltd.
A Penguin Company
80 Strand, London, WC2R 0RL, England
Penguin Books Australia Ltd, 250 Camberwell Road,
Camberwell, Victoria 3124, Australia
New York, Canada, India, New Zealand, South Africa
2 4 6 8 10 9 7 5 3 1
© Eric Hill, 2004
Eric Hill has asserted his moral rights under the
Copyright, Designs and Patents Act of 1988
All rights reserved
Planned and produced by Ventura Publishing Ltd
80 Strand, London WC2R 0RL
Printed in Italy

Spot's
Show and
Tell

Eric Hill

Spot and his friends arrived at school bright and early.

"Good morning, everyone,"
said Miss Bear.
"Good morning,
Miss Bear,"
everyone replied.

When everyone was settled,
Miss Bear asked, "Does anyone
have anything special for
Show and Tell today?"

Helen and Tom both put their
hands up.

Miss Bear asked Helen to come up first.

Helen held up her pink ballet shoes for everyone to see. They had lovely ribbons to keep them on her feet.

"Every week I go to ballet class," said Helen. "Next week we're doing a concert and I'm going to be a flower!"

Everyone thought Helen's ballet shoes were very special. They all clapped. Helen was very happy.

Next it was Tom's turn.
"I've brought my new kite,"
said Tom. "It's very special.
My dad helped me to make it.
We used special paper, wooden
sticks and glue. We're going to
fly it on Saturday."

Everyone thought Tom's kite was
wonderful and they all clapped.
Tom was very happy.

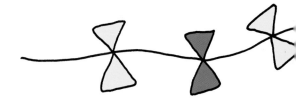

Later that morning, it was time for painting. Spot and Steve shared an easel.

"I'm going to bring something for Show and Tell tomorrow," said Spot.

"Me too," said Steve. "But I'm not sure what to bring."
"Neither am I," said Spot. "We'll have to think hard, won't we?"

That afternoon, Steve was going to Spot's house to play. Sally picked Spot and Steve up and they all walked home together.

Steve saw a bright orange autumn leaf on the grass and he picked it up.

"Maybe I'll take this for Show and Tell tomorrow," he said. "It's a lovely colour!"

19

When they got back, Spot and Steve played cars in Spot's room.

"My car collection is special,"
Spot said to Steve. "Maybe I'll
take my cars to Show and
Tell tomorrow."
"That's a good idea," said Steve.

At bedtime, Spot was still
thinking about Show and Tell.

Suddenly, he had a great idea.
"I know what I want to take to
Show and Tell tomorrow," said
Spot. "It's very, very special."
Spot whispered something
to Sally.

"That sounds perfect!" said Sally,
and she kissed Spot goodnight.
"Sweet dreams, Spot!"

The next morning, Spot was
smiling and cheerful when he met
Steve on the way to school.
"Have you got something for
Show and Tell?" asked Steve.
"Yes," said Spot. "And it's very,
very special. Have you got
something?"
"Yes," said Steve, happily.
"And it's very special too."

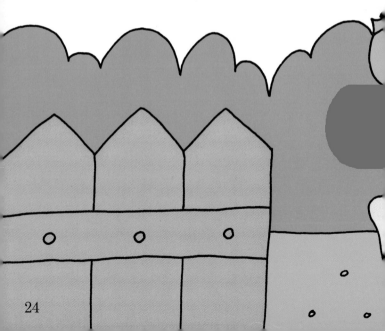

At school, Miss Bear asked if anyone had brought something special for Show and Tell.

Spot and Steve put their hands up and Miss Bear asked them to come to the front of the class.

"I'd like to show the picture
I painted of my friend Spot!"
said Steve.

Spot laughed.
"And I'd like to show the picture
I painted of my friend Steve,"
said Spot.

Everyone clapped, even Miss Bear!
Spot and Steve were very,
very happy!